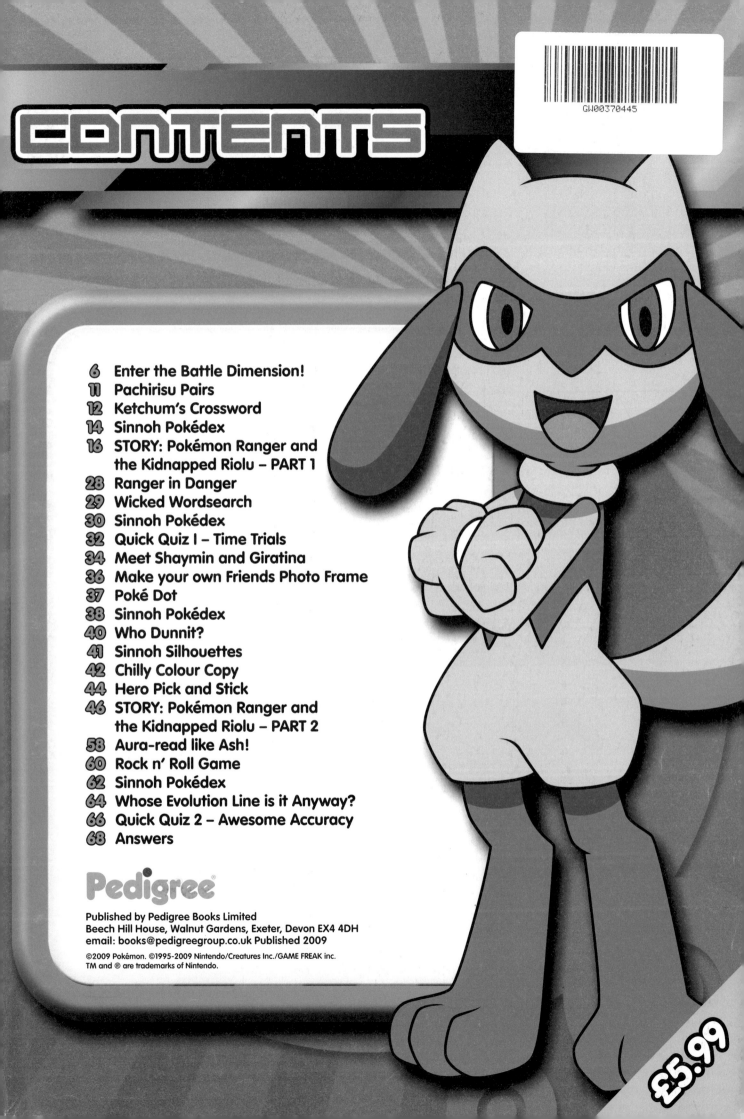

CONTENTS

Pedigree®

Published by Pedigree Books Limited
Beech Hill House, Walnut Gardens, Exeter, Devon EX4 4DH
email: books@pedigreegroup.co.uk Published 2009

©2009 Pokémon. ©1995-2009 Nintendo/Creatures Inc./GAME FREAK inc.
TM and ® are trademarks of Nintendo.

£5.99

GW00370445

ASH

ALTHOUGH still so young, Ash Ketchum is already well on his way to becoming the greatest Pokémon Trainer in the world. From humble beginnings in Pallet Town he's progressed through the regions of Kanto, Johto and Hoenn; battling Gym Leaders, capturing wild Pokémon and increasing in knowledge and skill.

Ash is not without flaws and his unerring self-belief can occasionally lead him to make errors of judgement. He has also been beaten in battle several times by rival Trainer Paul. Luckily our hero is always willing to learn from his mistakes! Ash has an abundance of great virtues including courage, determination and loyalty – qualities he displays to both humans and Pokémon.

In fact, many say the secret to Ash's success lies in the respect he shows to all Pokémon. Many even choose to follow him willingly rather than wait to be caught by him. Now in Sinnoh – an exotic and challenging region, Ash is as always primed for battle and ready for a new adventure!

PIKACHU

PIKACHU and Ash have a very special relationship. Not only are they battle partners, they are the best of friends! The pair are inseparable, each willingly putting their life on the line for the other one.

Things weren't always so friendly however. The electric Pokémon did not take to the young Trainer at first and stubbornly ignored his request to be transported in his Poké Ball. Even now Pikachu continues to travel on Ash's shoulder.

Everything changed when Ash saved Pikachu from attack by a flock of wild Spearow and these days a battle rarely takes place without his involvement. The sparky Pokémon's trademark moves include the awesome Volt Tackle and Thunderbolt. Powered by the electricity stored in its cheeks, Ash's friend can channel enough power to floor even the toughest of challengers.

BROCK

THERE are two very different sides to Brock. The first is a nurturing character that takes care of every injured Pokémon he comes across. A perfect gentleman, Brock provides a fatherly role model to Ash. The other Brock is a cool operator – an intelligent ex-Gym Leader who can call on a vast knowledge of Pokémon, their behaviour and attributes. Brock is so clued-up he often provides an answer for Ash before his young friend has time to consult his Pokédex!

Ash first met his friend in Pewter City Gym where Brock was working whilst dreaming of greater things. He'd always wanted to become a Breeder but in his father's absence he'd stayed home to care for his brothers and sisters. When Brock's father returned, he happily joined Ash on his journey, delighted to be able to follow his own path at last.

DAWN

UNLIKE her two buddies, Dawn is not set on becoming a Trainer or a Breeder. She wants a career as a Pokémon Co-ordinator, just like her mother before her. This involves entering her Pokémon in contests rather than pitting them against others in combat. However, although her heart lies elsewhere, when necessary Dawn is more than willing to earn her stripes in battle. In Veilstone City she proved her worth by offering to go up against rookie Gym Leader Maylene in order to help her regain her confidence.

In Sinnoh, Dawn's main travelling companion is Piplup. The loyal creature's amazing Bubble Beam move has defeated countless foes on many occasions. Dawn has an eye for fashion and loves to look her best at all times. She adores meeting up with other girls in order to admire their style and talk clothes.

TEAM ROCKET

JESSIE, JAMES AND THEIR UNIQUE TALKING POKÉMON MEOWTH are always on hand to throw a spanner in the works. Team Rocket plan to take over the world using whatever foul means necessary! Their mysterious boss Giovanni has also specifically requested that the trio steal Ash's extraordinary Pikachu.

The bumbling threesome constantly try to obstruct Ash and his friends using a series of increasingly madcap schemes. Luckily the villains' lack of planning and hugely over-inflated egos mean that their feeble attempts always end in disaster.

Wherever our heroes find themselves, be it in a canyon or on a mountain pass, Team Rocket is never far away. Whether the tricky trio are skulking behind bushes, hiding on rooftops or hovering overhead in their oh-so-obvious hot air balloon (emblazoned with a huge image of Meowth), you can be sure of one thing – they're eavesdropping on every word…

PACHIRISU PAIRS

Check out these Pachirisu! Only two of them are identical, but can you use your powers of observation to work out which ones they are? Circle the matching pair with a pen or a pencil.

KETCHUM'S CROSSWORD

A keen mind is a Pokémon Trainer's most important asset. Why not do some brain training with Ash's crossword? Check out the cunning clues opposite then use your knowledge plus the information contained in this book to help you fill in the answers.

ACROSS

1. Word meaning devious, describing Team Rocket. (3)

2. and 4. The awesome move that Donphan uses it to clear a cave of rocks in the story. (4,3)

3. A fish-like Pokémon that has a tail which shines brightly in the dark after exposure to the sun. (7)

5. Your hero's surname. (7)

6.

This electric/ghost Pokémon has a body made of plasma and can cause electronic devices to malfunction. (5)

7.

This psychic Pokémon can wipe people's memory and is known as 'The Being of Knowledge'. (4)

8. Bug/Flying Pokémon with wings that can cause injury. (7)

9. Friendly Normal-Type Pokémon with a tail shaped like a hand. (5)

10.

Cute pink Pokémon that evolves into Clefairy. (6)

DOWN

1. Glalie and Froslass's first evolution. (7)

2. Female responsible for keeping law and order in the world of Pokémon. (7,5)

3. Something Brock does whenever he meets an attractive young lady. He falls _ _ _ _ _ _. (2,4)

4. The region that Ash and his friends are currently journeying through. (6)

5. A budding Pokémon Breeder and Ash's great friend. (5)

6. The phrase Ranger Kellyn says when using his Vatonage Styler to harness a wild Pokémon's power. 'Capture _ _'. (2)

7.

A fatter version of its first form Glameow, this Pokémon uses its size to barge into the nests of others. (7)

8. Bat-like Flying Pokémon that hangs upside down in trees. (7)

9. Rock-Type resembling a snake in form, that can travel underground. (4)

10.

This Bug-Type steals honey from Combee. (6)

11. Jessie, James and Meowth always end up blasting _ _ _.(3)

SINNOH POKÉDEX

PROBOPASS

TYPE:	ROCK/STEEL
ABILITY:	STURDY/MAGNET PULL
HEIGHT:	1.4m
WEIGHT:	340.0kg

Evolved from Nosepass, this Rock/Steel Pokémon emits a strong magnetic force. The three Mini-Noses on its sides are detachable and can move separately under the main unit's control.

CRESSELIA

TYPE:	PSYCHIC
ABILITY:	LEVITATE
HEIGHT:	1.5m
WEIGHT:	85.6kg

Cresselia possesses the natural ability to calm and soothe anguish in humans. Its wings release particles that create a shining halo around it, representing the arc of the crescent moon.

FINNEON

TYPE:	WATER
ABILITY:	SWIFT SWIM/STORM DRAIN
HEIGHT:	0.4m
WEIGHT:	7.0kg

Known as the 'Beautifly of the Sea', Finneon's tail fins are solar-powered! When exposed to sunlight during the day, they will glow brightly at night. Finneon evolves into Lumineon.

RIOLU

TYPE:	FIGHTING
ABILITY:	STEADFAST/INNER FOCUS
HEIGHT:	0.7m
WEIGHT:	20.2kg

Evolving to Lucario, this blue, dog-like Pokémon gives out an aura which alerts others to its feelings and emotions. Riolu is renowned for its strength and unenviable endurance in battle.

POKÉMON RANGER AND THE KIDNAPPED
PART 1

A VAST AND MOUNTAINOUS EXPANSE OF FOREST AWAITS OUR HEROES AS THEY CONTINUE THEIR JOURNEY THROUGH THE SINNOH REGION. THE TERRAIN IS WILD AND BEAUTIFUL, BUT OLD ADVERSARIES LURK AT EVERY TURN AND AN EXTRAORDINARY RIOLU LIES AT THE CENTRE OF AN EVIL PLOT...

Deep in the forest an explosion blew a hole in the walls of an imposing grey fortress. A blue Pokémon scrambled out towards a group of men in military uniforms and their Golem – The Rock/Ground type Pokémon responsible for the blast. Three heavily armed guards, accompanied by an angry-looking man in a white coat peered out through the rubble, scanning the darkness for the escapee.

"RX1 is a priceless research tool! Get Riolu back at once," yelled the man in white, ordering his guards after the fleeing Pokémon.
Suddenly an armoured van screeched up and moments later soldiers were speeding away with Riolu safe in the back. The Pokémon had not been saved however – it had been thrown out of the frying pan and into the fire.
"Excellent! Riolu finally belongs to me!" chuckled a sinister figure in the back seat, the criminal behind Riolu's latest capture.
"Promising to help Riolu doesn't mean we'd send it home," chuckled the driver. His laughter was cut short as a bang sent the truck skidding off the road. Riolu had overheard and escaped again, blasting through the reinforced metal.
"So this is its power," gasped the man.
"I must have Riolu for my own!"

RIOLU!

A few hours later Ash was travelling through the forest with his friends when he felt a searing pain in his head. "Ash, is something wrong?" asked Dawn.
"Nope," said Ash, confused by the images which had just flashed through his mind. There was a rustling of bushes and a Pokémon stumbled onto the path.
"Whoa!" bellowed Ash. "What's that?"
As usual Brock knew the answer. "It's a Riolu!"
Ash pulled out his Pokédex.

"Now I understand what happened to my head!" added Ash.

Brock noticed a cut on Riolu's arm. Ash bent forward to help the Pokémon, but was thrown across the ground by a powerful orb. Luckily the Trainer was more overawed than hurt by the blow.
"That was an Aura Sphere for sure!" Brock told a surprised Dawn. "That move's normally learned after Riolu evolves into Lucario, but not this time!"
"That Riolu must be really special!" gasped Dawn.
Ash tried again to tend to the injured Pokémon, who responded by throwing another terrifying Aura Sphere in his direction.

RIOLU
THE EMANATION POKÉMON

WHEN SAD OR SCARED, RIOLU'S AURA BECOMES STRONGER AS A WAY OF SIGNALING TO ITS ALLIES

"Don't worry I'll handle this!" said a young, brown-haired boy appearing from nowhere and deftly deflecting Riolu's next blow. Riolu turned and ran for the undergrowth, with the boy in hot pursuit.
"I wonder who that could be…?" wondered Dawn.
"C'mon guys," ordered Ash. "We can't just stand here and do nothing when Riolu needs help!" He sped after Riolu and the stranger, with Brock and Dawn running behind.

Lurking behind some bushes, Team Rocket had seen enough.
"An Aura Sphere-toting Riolu is one rare and power-packed Pokémon," said James.
"Yeah! An' dat's da kind a' power we need ta pack!' added Meowth.
"We can't allow Riolu to languish with those lame losers!" screeched Jessie.
Up ahead, Ash, Dawn, Brock and their new friend were huddled in the undergrowth watching Riolu standing on the branch of a tree.

"Is that your Riolu?" asked Dawn.
The boy shook his head.
Ash looked confused. "So is it wild?"
"Nope," replied the boy. "All Riolu wants to do is get back home."
Suddenly two enormous armoured vehicles crashed into the clearing directly below the frightened Pokémon.

Pikachu and the Crobats flew into battle.
All at once Ash, Pikachu and J's crew were
sent flying by Riolu.
"So that's the famous Aura Sphere," marvelled
one henchman, picking himself up. "Riolu's ours!"
said the other.

"I won't allow it," called a stern voice.
It was the boy, clicking a contraption attached
to his wrist.
"It's a Vatonage Styler!" said Brock.
"Then he's a…" trailed Dawn.
"…Pokémon Ranger!" finished Ash.
Skilfully the boy trained his Styler on an Ariados
that was dangling in a nearby tree.
"Capture…ON!" he yelled. "Vatonage!
Capture complete."
The Ariados succumbed to his will at once.
The boy prepared for his next move.
"Use String Shot!" he directed.
The attacking Crobats found themselves tied in a
bundle. The Ranger captured a nearby Nincada
and ordered him to dig a hole beneath the men,
who fell straight in. "Awesome!" whistled Ash.

"That's Pokémon Hunter J's goon squad!"
yelled Dawn above the racket.
Two bulky men lumbered from the ship,
directing their Crobats to attack Riolu.
"Retrieve the target!" shouted one.
"Those thugs are after Riolu!" whispered Brock.
This was too much for Ash. Always ready to
defend a Pokémon in peril, he sprang from
the bushes with Pikachu on his shoulder.
"Pikachu," he shouted. "Use Thunderbolt!"

Dawn was totally impressed.
"Wow! Seeing a Pokémon Ranger in action up close and personal like this is so cool!"
"He's not an ordinary one either," said Brock excitedly. "He's a Top Ranger!"
Brock explained that the title is given only to those skilled enough to use a Vatonage Capture Styler.

As the friends looked on, the Ranger pulled a tiny wooden doll out of his pocket and handed it to the nervous Pokémon. It was the image of Riolu.
"You see you can trust me," he said gently, placing the doll in a pouch and tying it around Riolu's neck.

Picking up Riolu and urging Ash, Brock and Dawn to follow, the Ranger began running deeper into the forest.
"So you came out here to help out that Riolu?" asked Ash.
"Right!" answered the Ranger.
"The name's Kellyn!"
The friends panted their introductions.
"Hi, I'm Ash!"
"My name's Dawn!"
"Nice to meet you, I'm Brock."

From their vantage point in the bushes, Team Rocket watched in disbelief.
"First we get pre-empted by a pack of Pokémon Hunter henchmen," moaned James. "Then we get upstaged by a Pokémon Ranger!"
Meowth was more optimistic. "When those heavy weights want what we want we're barking up da right tree!"
"That Hunter Hussy J is going to pay!" spat Jessie. "I'll turn the tables on her so fast her head will spin."

Meanwhile Kellyn was attending to Riolu's wounds.
"You'll be feeling better in no time!" he smiled. Riolu backed away.
"It looks like Riolu's suffered through some tough stuff," said Kellyn sadly.
"Maybe that's why it attacked Ash," suggested Brock. "It's gonna take time before it can trust people again," nodded Kellyn.

Riolu took out the little doll and gazed at it fondly.
"This is a gift from the man who raised it," explained Kellyn.
He didn't need to continue – Ash was seeing everything through Riolu's aura projections. In his mind's eye he watched Riolu practising its moves while an old man carved it a doll before the scene switched to the Pokémon being snatched by research scientists and code-named Project RX1.

"That doll's worth more to you than anything, right Riolu?" said Ash, opening his eyes. Dawn looked confused. "It used its aura to tell us that?"

"Riolu transmits all of its emotions and memories in this way," explained Brock.
"All living things have their own unique aura," agreed Kellyn. "Ash, it looks like your Aura and Riolu's are a perfect match!"

"I'll help get ya home safe Riolu," promised Ash. "Don't worry about Hunter J."

Just then Kellyn's Capture Styler buzzed. He flipped up a screen to reveal a girl, also in Ranger's uniform.
"Solana!" exclaimed Ash.
"Ash and Pikachu!" replied the girl.
"It's been a long time…."
"Wow a girl Ranger!" gushed Dawn.
"And with such awesome clothes!"
Brock jostled to the microphone.
"I hope you didn't forget little ole me Solana?"
"Of course not!" answered the Ranger.
"Still working to be a Breeder?"

"Yes, but now I'm also working on getting you to use your Capture Styler to capture my heart!" Brock's slushy speech was cut short by Croagunk. The irritated Pokémon stepped forward and gave his master a toxic jab in the rear!

Before signing off Solana told Kellyn that she and Officer Jenny were looking for Hunter J's captive. Kellyn nodded. "Riolu's under our protection and we're heading towards the rendezvous coordinates."

Suddenly a huge object blotted out the sun.

"It's Hunter J's ship!" yelled Dawn.

"Everybody needs to stay calm and do just what I say!" warned Kellyn, leading the group down a wooded bank towards a fast-flowing river.

In the cockpit of her airship, J was interrogating her hapless crew.

"Forgive me," grovelled one henchman. "Our target managed to escape with a Top Pokémon Ranger."

"Was it Kellyn?" sneered J.

"The henchman nodded. "And he was being helped by a group of young punks!"

"Not them again!" shouted J. "So you're saying they're your excuse for failure?"

"Negative. We still intend to retrieve the target!"

Miles below the airship, Ash and his friends were huddled in a boat being towed by Piplup and Buizel. Kellyn was explaining to them why Riolu was so special.

"This Paradise Kingdom is Riolu's home," he began. "Its official title is 'Inheritor of the Aura'. Each royal generation uses the Pokémon's aura to protect the kingdom. It gets passed on and on from generation to generation… this Riolu's the next in line."

"So that's why Riolu can use Aurasphere," exclaimed Ash.

"Riolu was kidnapped twice by people planning to use its power for evil purposes," nodded Kellyn.

"And now this – hunted by a Pokémon Hunter!" replied Brock. "No wonder it doesn't trust anyone outside its kingdom."

Suddenly Ash yelled as the boat was overturned by four fearsome Sharpedo.

"Those belong to Hunter J!" gasped Brock. "They've found us!"

Spying a Floatzel in the water ahead, Kellyn was quick to respond.
"Capture On!" he said, temporarily harnessing the power of the Water-type. Floatzel valiantly began to tow the group to safety, but not before Hunter J's crew had ordered their Sharpedo to mount an Aquajet attack.
Clinging to Ash's cap, Pikachu bought some time by countering with his Thunderbolt move.

"J!" screamed Ash, as the Hunter floated into view atop an enormous Salamence.
"I'm taking Riolu," she announced coldly.
The cruel bounty hunter turned Salamence's Hyperbeam on the group in the water. Dawn ordered Piplup to respond with Bubblebeam. Next Kellyn added Floatzel's Water Gun, which doused Salamence's beam and finally unbalanced J.

Enraged, J blasted the canyon behind in her retreat, sending boulders raining down on the group. The friends narrowly dodged being hit. "She's gone," whispered Kellyn at last, but then he gasped in horror. Riolu was paddling rapidly downstream, desperately trying to catch the doll which had fallen into the water.

Ash, still clinging to Buizel and Pikachu, began frantically swimming after Riolu. Seconds later however, the lost Pokémon was swept over a towering waterfall and into the churning water below.
"Riolu's in trouble!" gasped Ash. "Dive!"
Buizel swam down and down until Ash spotted the unconscious Pokémon. The Trainer grabbed it tightly and pulled hard.

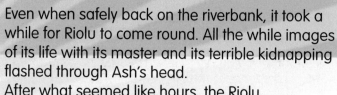

Even when safely back on the riverbank, it took a while for Riolu to come round. All the while images of its life with its master and its terrible kidnapping flashed through Ash's head.
After what seemed like hours, the Riolu opened its eyes.
"I'm so glad you're awake Riolu," smiled Ash.
"We were worried!"
He hugged the Pokémon tightly, then handed the delighted Riolu its wooden doll.
"This belongs ta you! Take good care of it."
Upstream J and her henchmen were re-grouping, desperate to launch a new attack.

Round the corner Team Rocket were digging themselves a hole in more ways than one. "I know this is what we do," asked James, shovelling hard. "But will a pit trap bring down Hunter J?"

"Like rain from the sky!" said Jessie.

It took Meowth to notice that the tables had in fact already turned – and not in their favour. J was fast approaching on her fire-breathing Salamence! "We gotta move fast!"

The three jumped into their hole to escape Salamence's flames.

"It's time to use our pit digging expertise for self-preservation," added Jessie as J's enormous dragon-like Pokémon began to set the entire forest alight.

The criminal swept past Team Rocket, directing Salamence back towards Ash and his friends. "I warned you to stay out of my way!" screamed J.

Salamence's flames licked the ground around him and his friends, encircling them in a raging ring of fire.

"I'm takin' care of Riolu," answered Ash defiantly. "And you just ran outta luck!"

WILL ASH AND HIS FRIENDS REALLY BE ABLE TO SAFELY RETURN RIOLU BACK TO ITS KINGDOM AND ITS TRUE DESTINY? TURN TO PAGE 46 TO FIND OUT!

RANGER IN DANGER

Oh no! Ranger Kellyn has been injured by a wild Murkrow and, as Sinnoh legend has it, something ominous has indeed happened – Jessie has made off with his Vatonage Capture Styler. Can you show Ash the way to retrieve it for his new friend? Use your finger to help you trace the correct path.

WICKED WORDSEARCH

Can you find Ash's dastardly opponents, enemies and rivals hidden within the word gird below?

B	T	U	O	U	E	F	D	W	R	O
E	E	J	L	U	A	P	D	J	S	Q
N	F	X	O	T	S	U	D	P	E	U
I	F	C	F	J	B	A	A	S	V	D
V	U	H	A	A	M	J	Z	A	I	W
I	B	M	I	M	R	E	P	K	P	M
N	B	A	R	E	A	S	O	S	E	E
R	O	N	T	S	E	S	W	W	R	O
A	W	N	P	Z	P	I	V	A	T	A
C	U	A	F	T	M	E	J	R	E	H
H	I	N	N	A	V	O	I	G	S	S

- [ ] **GIOVANNI**
- [✓] **JAMES**
- [✓] **CARNIVINE**
- [✓] **HUNTER J**
- [ ] **WOBBUFFET**
- [ ] **SEVIPER**
- [ ] **MEOWTH**
- [ ] **JESSIE**
- [ ] **DUSTOX**
- [ ] **PAUL**

ABOMASNOW

TYPE:	GRASS/ICE
ABILITY:	SNOW WARNING
HEIGHT:	2.2m
WEIGHT:	135.5kg

Abomasnow can withstand the fiercest mountain storms by wedging its feet down into the ground. It evolves from Snover and is undoubtedly the famous 'yeti' of legend.

DUSKNOIR

TYPE:	GHOST
ABILITY:	PRESSURE
HEIGHT:	2.2m
WEIGHT:	106.6kg

Spooky Dusknoir is the last in Duskull's evolutionary chain. It uses its antennae to pick up commands broadcast from the world of spirits, ordering it to pick up humans.

CROBAT

TYPE:	POISON/FLYING
ABILITY:	INNER FOCUS
HEIGHT:	1.8m
WEIGHT:	75.0kg

This mainly nocturnal Pokémon has four arched wings, which enable it to fly with speed and stealth. Its sharp yellow eyes enhance its night vision. Crobat is the final evolution of Zubat.

BUIZEL

TYPE:	WATER
ABILITY:	SWIFT SWIM
HEIGHT:	0.7m
WEIGHT:	29.5kg

Found in Sinnoh's waters, this Pokémon has a flotation sac that resembles an inflatable collar. This buoyancy allows it to swim with its head above the water even in the roughest conditions.

QUICK QUIZ
PART 1
TIME TRIALS

For a Trainer, Breeder or Co-ordinator to thrive in the world of Pokémon, they need to have a combination of speed and accuracy. The first part of this quiz has been especially designed to test how quick your reactions really are!

Time yourself as you take the tick test. Afterwards add 5 seconds on to your final time for every question you got wrong. Your aim is to complete it in less than 60 seconds!

1 Only Top Rangers are allowed to use a Vatonage Capture Styler.
YES ☑   NO ☐

2 Glaceon is a Grass-Type Pokémon.
YES ☐
NO ☑

3 Ash's surname is Ketchup.
YES ☐   NO ☑

4 Giratina dwells in a reverse world.
YES ☑   NO ☐

5 Pikachu travels in a Poké Ball.
YES ☐
NO ☑

6 Mamoswine has one giant tusk protruding from its head.
YES ☐   NO ☑

7 Nurse Joy is often aided by a Pokémon called Happiny.

YES ☑ NO ☐

8 Buneary slams its foe by sharply unrolling its coiled ears.

YES ☑
NO ☐

9 Brock and Ash met in Pallet Town.

YES ☑ NO ☐

10 Gastrodon are either blue and green with yellow markings or black with yellow markings.

YES ☐ NO ☑

11 Bronzor's next evolution is Budew.

YES ☐
NO ☑

12 Dawn's preferred travel companion in Sinnoh is Piplup.

YES ☑ NO ☐

13 Buizel stays afloat by blowing water through its nostrils.

YES ☐
NO ☑

14 Pikachu stores electricity in its thunderbolt-shaped tail.

YES ☐ NO ☑

15 Gliscor can fly.

YES ☑ NO ☐

OVER 90 SECONDS

You've still much to learn, but everyone has to start somewhere! Ash has made many errors on his travels and each one has helped shape him into the Trainer he is today. Read back through the answers and commit them to memory to broaden your knowledge for next time.

60 TO 90 SECONDS

A promising start! Brush up on the questions you got wrong, then leave the quiz for a week and redo it. See if you can better your score second time round. The best Trainers store Pokémon info in their brains til they need it most!

UNDER 60 SECONDS

CONGRATULATIONS. You're one quick customer and are showing great potential to become a Pokémon Master! You must have answered like lightning, and not incurred penalties to have come out with this super score. If you're ready to further test your accuracy, turn to the quiz on pages 66-67.

MEET SHAYMIN
(LAND FORME)

PREPARE TO MEET TWO VERY DIFFERENT SINNOH-DWELLING POKÉMON. ASH, BROCK AND DAWN COULDN'T BELIEVE THEIR LUCK WHEN THEY ENCOUNTERED THESE TWO SPECIES ON THEIR TRAVELS. BET YOU'LL LOVE THEM TOO!

Shaymin is a tiny, Grass-Type Pokémon found in meadows or flowery dwells. It has two Formes – the Land Forme looks rather like a small hedgehog and the Sky Forme is deer-like in appearance. The Land Forme of Shaymin is timid and easily frightened, curling itself up into a ball whenever threatened. Its grassy spines and floral markings allow it to blend into its surroundings until danger has passed. The Pokémon's Sky Forme is more fearless and happy to battle foes that threaten its habitat or food source.

Shaymin has a unique purity that enables it to breath in dirty fumes and exhale pristine, fresh air. It is also believed to have transformed several urban areas of wasteland in Sinnoh into lush meadows.

AND GIRATINA
(ALTERED FORME)

On the other hand, Giratina the Ghost-Dragon Pokémon lives in the mysterious Reverse World – a realm mirroring the real world. Little is known about this parallel dimension, but it is said that here Giratina moves in its Origin Forme. The remarkable Pokémon can be characterised by a body covered in gold spikes. The Altered Forme is even more awe-inspiring with six powerful legs replacing some spikes and a greater wing span.

Legend has it that that once a Shaymin stumbled onto the path of a Giratina locked in battle with Dialga, believing the ancient deity to have polluted its home. The intensity of the combat dragged the Shaymin into Giratina's Reverse World, provoking a catastrophic series of events which would be felt by all Sinnoh's inhabitants…

TAKE A LOOK AT THE PROFILES OPPOSITE TO FAMILIARISE YOURSELF WITH THESE POKÉMON. YOU'RE SURE TO HEAR ABOUT THEM OFTEN FROM NOW ON!

SHAYMIN

LAND FORME

TYPE:	GRASS
ABILITY:	NATURAL CURE
HEIGHT:	0.2m
WEIGHT:	2.1kg

SKY FORME

TYPE:	GRASS/FLYING
ABILITY:	SERENE GRACE
HEIGHT:	0.4m
WEIGHT:	5.2kg

GIRATINA

ORIGIN FORME

TYPE:	GHOST/DRAGON
ABILITY:	LEVITATE
HEIGHT:	6.9m
WEIGHT:	650.0kg

ALTERED FORME

TYPE:	GHOST/DRAGON
ABILITY:	PRESSURE
HEIGHT:	4.5m
WEIGHT:	750.0kg

MAKE YOUR OWN FRIENDS PHOTO FRAME

Ash, Dawn and Brock are the closest of friends, sharing amazing adventures and having great fun together. Why not use this simple photo frame make-it to create a lasting memory of you and your best buddies? You could keep it for yourself or give it to them as a gift.

You will need: Scissors; Thick white card; PVA glue; Pencil; A favourite photo or drawing that fits within the border; Sticky back plastic.

1. Ask an adult to help you cut or trace the frame border from the bottom of this page.
2. Carefully glue the border onto a sheet of card to make it more sturdy.
3. Use scissors to score into the centre of the mounted border, then cut out the inside area of the frame.
4. Now place the frame onto a second piece of card. Take a pencil and draw round the edge to measure out a backing board for the photo frame.
5. Cut the backing board out.
6. Glue your picture in place on the backing board, then cover it with sticky back plastic.
7. Glue your card frame on top of the picture and put it to one side.
8. Cut or trace the frame stand from this page. Mount it onto card to make it more sturdy then score and fold along the dotted lines.
9. Finally glue your frame stand onto your backing board then put it up for everyone to admire!

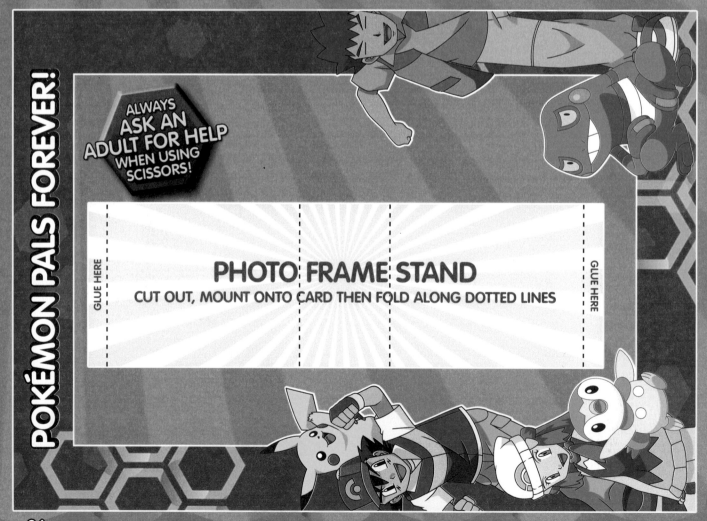

POKÉMON PALS FOREVER!

ALWAYS ASK AN ADULT FOR HELP WHEN USING SCISSORS!

GLUE HERE

PHOTO FRAME STAND
CUT OUT, MOUNT ONTO CARD THEN FOLD ALONG DOTTED LINES

GLUE HERE

©2009 Pokémon. ©1995-2009 Nintendo/Creatures Inc./GAME FREAK inc.
TM and © are trademarks of Nintendo

POKÉ DOT

Which awesome Pokémon lurks here? Join the dots to discover who it is. Here's a clue – when it extends its wings it looks like a jet plane, but it can actually fly even faster! When you've finished, use felt-tip pens or pencils to colour it in!

SINNOH POKÉDEX

GLISCOR

TYPE:	GROUND/FLYING
ABILITY:	HYPER CUTTER/SAND VEIL
HEIGHT:	2.0m
WEIGHT:	42.5kg

This fanged Pokémon boasts sharp claws and a dangerous tail with which to lash its foes. It is a master of surprise and hangs silently in trees waiting for unsuspecting prey to pass by.

FLOATZEL

TYPE:	WATER
ABILITY:	SWIFT SWIM
HEIGHT:	1.0m
WEIGHT:	33.5kg

The evolved form of Buizel, this Water-type has an even more advanced flotation sac which surrounds its body. Because of its attributes, Floatzel often assists in the rescue of drowning humans.

PORYGON-Z

TYPE:	NORMAL
ABILITY:	ADAPTABILITY/DOWNLOAD
HEIGHT:	0.9m
WEIGHT:	34.0kg

Developed from Porygon and Porygon2, Porygon-Z is equipped with extra software to enhance behaviour, but it has acted very strangely since the modification took place. It can be quite unpredictable.

GOLEM

TYPE:	ROCK/GROUND
ABILITY:	ROCK HEAD/STURDY
HEIGHT:	1.4m
WEIGHT:	300.0kg

This heavyweight Rock-Type has a boulder-like body so tough that even dynamite can't destroy it. It sheds its hide once a year and evolves from Geodude to Graveler before reaching its current form.

DRAPION

TYPE:	POISON/DARK
ABILITY:	BATTLE ARMOUR/SNIPER
HEIGHT:	1.3m
WEIGHT:	61.5kg

This Pokémon releases poison from the tips of its claws to finish off its victims. Most prey however, have already been crushed to dust by pincers so strong they can reduce a car to scrap in seconds.

GALLADE

TYPE:	PSYCHIC/FIGHTING
ABILITY:	STEADFAST
HEIGHT:	1.6m
WEIGHT:	52.0kg

One of Kirlia's two evolutions, Gallade makes a formidable opponent. It uses extending blades attached to its elbows to overcome its foes. It also has spikes behind its eyes.

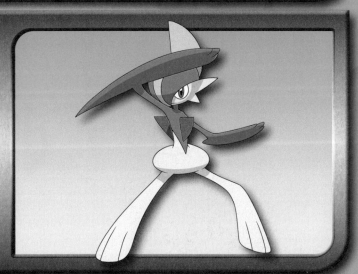

WHO DUNNIT?

One of these five Pokémon has been causing trouble in Sinnoh. Can you help Officer Jenny track them down, just by using your detective skills? Look at the statements below one by one, apply them to the line up and after each statement, eliminate one suspect. At the end you'll be left with a single Pokémon.

GLISCOR	STUNKY	TENTACRUEL	PURUGLY	DRAPION

1. **I do not have the letter 'K' in my name.**

2. **I cannot fly.**

3. **I am a Poison-Type Pokémon.**

4. **I have powerful claws.**

Which Pokémon is Officer Jenny chasing?

Stick

SINNOH SILHOUETTES

In the forests and mountains of Sinnoh, dense trees and caverns provide countless hiding places for the more elusive Pokémon species. Ash, Brock and Dawn have spied the shadows of five wild Pokémon, but can you work out which ones they've come across?

Draw a line between each shadow and their correct name.

1

2

3

4

5

A REGIGIGAS

B PALKIA

C DIALGA

D MAGMORTAR

E GIRATINA

DID YOU KNOW?

Magmortar can blast molten fireballs of over 2,000 degrees C out of the end of its arms!

CHILLY COLOUR COPY

These frosty friends are Sinnoh Ice-Types Glaceon and Froslass. Can you copy them carefully into the empty grids then colour them in using cool blues, purples and greys?

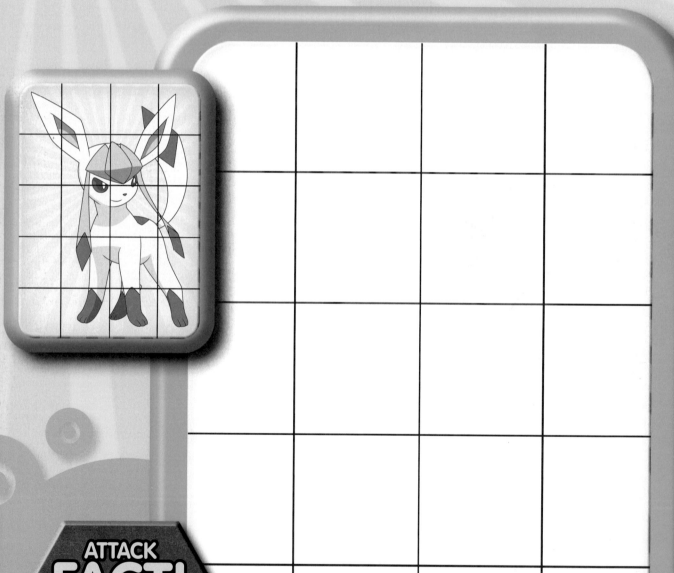

ATTACK FACT!
When threatened Glaceon freezes its hair so that its fur stands up in sharp spikes all over its body.

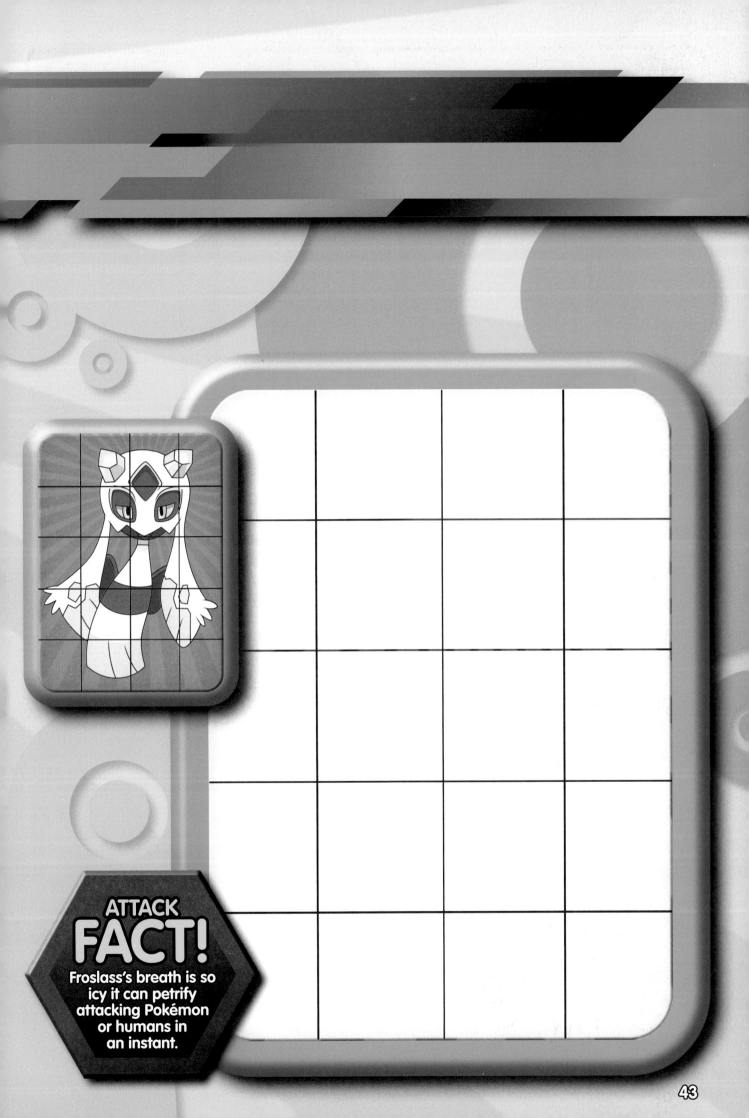

ATTACK
FACT!
Froslass's breath is so
icy it can petrify
attacking Pokémon
or humans in
an instant.

HERO
PICK AND STICK

My favourite Pokémon Hero is ....

because ....

....

....

....

....

Everyone loves a hero and the world of Pokémon provides many inspirational characters. Do you aspire to be a fearless Trainer like Ash, an expert Breeder like Brock or a graceful Co-ordinator like their friend Dawn?

Use the space opposite to draw and colour in your favourite character – pick out their sticker from the centre pages to guide you. Now write down just why they inspire you. Start by describing your favourite battle or event, or make a list of the adjectives (describing words) from the Poké Ball below which sums them up best.

KNOWLEDGEABLE

FAST · WISE

THOUGHTFUL · CLEVER

SKILFUL · MATURE

KIND · PROUD

STYLISH · BRAVE

COURAGEOUS · FUNNY

HELPFUL

LOYAL

POKÉMON RANGER AND THE KIDNAPPED
PART 2

WHAT BEGAN AS A HARROWING ENCOUNTER WITH A POWERFUL RIOLU TURNED INTO AN ALLIANCE WITH TOP RANGER KELLYN WHEN HE AND OUR HEROES JOINED FORCES! CAN THE TEAM HELP RIOLU EVADE CAPTURE BY POKÉMON HUNTER J AND RETURN TO THE SAFETY OF HOME?

With fire raging all around, Ash was running out of options.

"Buizel, Water Gun!" he commanded, attempting to put out the flames streaming from Salamence's jaws.

Unfortunately it didn't work. The brave Trainer found himself and his beloved Pokémon trapped by a ring of fire.

"Enough," sneered Hunter J.

She trained her sights on Riolu then turned the poor Pokémon into stone.

"I spared Riolu the pain and suffering of the flames!" she mocked. "You should be grateful."

"You're not getting away with this!" yelled Ash, angrily clenching his fists.

J responded by ordering Salamence to set more sections of the forest alight.

46

RIOLU!

As the fires raged, dozens of panicked Pokémon streamed out of their woodland homes. Kellyn, Dawn and Brock were busy directing the herds towards the riverbank.

As usual the Ranger was calm.

"I need all of you to help!" he said, turning his attention to three huge Blastoise.

Kellyn directed his Vatonage styler on the tortoise-like Pokémon, instantly harnessing their Rain Dance power. The Blastoise began to create clouds that poured rain onto the flames, extinguishing each of them.

"You're all going to be just fine…" soothed Dawn.

"This is the work of Hunter J," said Kellyn.

"I'm worried about Ash and Riolu!"

With the fires out, J's henchmen moved in to pick up Riolu, encasing him in a glass bell jar. Team Rocket were at last driven out of their hole, which had now filled up with water.

"All right," moaned Jessie. "Who did the rain dance?"

"Not me! I was a bit preoccupied with treading water," retorted James.

Round the corner Ash and Pikachu were also emerging from an underground bolt-hole. "Thanks to you using Dig we're all safe and sound" he said to Chimchar. The young Trainer gratefully put the Fire-type Pokémon back in his Poké Ball.

Hearing a rumble, Ash ran towards the noise and was just in time to spot some henchmen loading Riolu onto J's ship. Without a thought for their own safety Ash and Pikachu sneaked on board.
Right behind them, Kellyn, Brock and Dawn were running hard through the forest. They could only stare in disbelief as the great ship suddenly rose above the trees and powered over their heads.
"That's Hunter J's ship!" cried Dawn.
"Does that mean they got Riolu?" asked Brock.

Inside the ship J was briefing her delighted client – the shadowy figure who had helped Riolu break-out of the research facility – on the success of her mission to re-kidnap the Pokémon.

Suddenly a furious Ash and Pikachu burst onto the flight deck.
"Let Riolu Go!" roared the Trainer at the top of his voice.
"Drapion, grab him now," replied J in a calm voice. "I've been aware of your little intrusion the whole time!"
Ash squirmed and struggled in Drapion's pincers. "Why didn't you do something before?" he choked.
"I wanted to punish you personally," sneered J. She was watched with amusement as Drapion dropped Ash and Pikachu through a hatch in the floor.

The best friends found themselves hurtling towards the ground at break-neck speed. "This could be it…" Ash yelled, hugging Pikachu to his chest.

Then, just as everything seemed lost, the frightened pair felt themselves being clutched by a set of enormous talons. "Got you Ash!" laughed Kellyn from his seat astride Staraptor.

The majestic Pokémon swooped to Earth carrying its relieved cargo beneath it.

As soon as he hit the ground, Ash started beating himself up.

"Riolu's with J because I messed up big time!" he wailed guiltily.

Kellyn tried to reassure him. "You shouldn't blame yourself. Don't worry, we'll save Riolu, for sure!"

Just then Dawn and Brock ran over, overjoyed to be reunited with Ash.

"I'm so glad you're all okay," panted Dawn.

Kellyn's Styler buzzed again.

It was Solana bearing bad news – J's evil client had escaped too. The gang were forced to consider the awful possibility that unless they could discover J and the client's rendezvous point, they would lose Riolu forever.

Spurred on by a challenge, Ash sprang into action.
He concentrated all his thoughts on Riolu and yelled into the distance.
"Tell me where you are RIOLU!" Nothing happened, so he tried again.
"If you can hear me somehow, tell me!" Suddenly an image flashed into his head showing Riolu in J's ship, deep inside a canyon.
"This way!" Ash beckoned.
"Riolu's this way."

"You realize if we follow in the Twerp's wake we'll come across Hunter J and Riolu in one fell swoop…" smiled Jessie as Team Rocket sneaked out of the shadows.
"Getting our paws on 'dat power-Pokeymon will kick us way up a notch!" squeaked Meowth.
"What do we do now our poor pit traps are water-logged?" asked James.

"We don't stand around and whine!" snapped Jessie. "Climb every mountain! Ford every stream! Rout Riolu!"
Still unaware that Team Rocket were trailing them, Ash, Dawn, Brock and Kellyn mounted a group of Dodrio and began riding furiously towards the canyon.
"Hang on Riolu!" cried Ash. "We're comin'!"

J's ship landed in the canyon and the bounty hunter eagerly awaited her client's arrival. She wanted to hurry up the handover of Riolu and more importantly her money. Meanwhile, Ash and his crew were moving ever closer.

"I still can't believe that Riolu's aura could reach Ash," said Dawn. "Not with Hunter J holding it prisoner!"

"That just goes to show how strong the connection is between Ash and Riolu!" smiled Brock.

"The aura's stronger so we must be getting really close now!" called Ash.

"I'm terribly sorry to keep you waiting Hunter J," said the client, arriving in the canyon and smiling at the sight of Riolu. J's henchman handed it over, still immobilised in stone and trapped in a glass case.

As they all turned to leave, a voice echoed down from the top of the canyon.

"We found ya J!" shouted Ash.

"A Pokémon Ranger?" the client gasped, freaking out at the sight of the Dodrio carrying Ash and Kellyn towards them.

"Riolu needs to return to its kingdom," ordered Kellyn. "Give it back or else!"

The client shook his head. "I'll give you nothing!"

Quick as lightning Ash summoned Staravia.
"Use Quick attack," he urged.
The bird swooped down on the client,
who dropped Riolu to the floor.
Hunter J quickly lost her nerve. "We've got
our money," she ordered. "Let's go!"
Ash's posse sped down the side of the
canyon on their Dodrio, just as the client
picked up Riolu again.
"I've finally got my hands on a Riolu that
uses Aurasphere!" he cried.
Behind him J's ship thundered skywards,
whipping sand up from the canyon floor.

Making use of the temporary diversion, Ash
called on Staravia's talents once more. The plucky
Pokémon slashed the tyres on the villain's vehicle
in one, neat fly-by. There was no getting away!
"Get him!" the client called to his men.
The soldiers began calling Pokémon from their
Poké Balls, ready to attack Ash. "Rhyorn!"
"Graveler!"
"Tyranitar!"
The list went on and on until a formidable
line-up appeared.

Still there was one more Pokémon to come – suddenly Fearow appeared in the sky! In one bound the client, clutching Riolu in one hand, managed to grab the Pokémon's claws and be lifted airborne. "I'll leave you to take care of them!" he barked at his soldiers below.

Just then Solana and officer Jenny screeched up on Jenny's motorbike. "Kellyn," called Solana. "Leave J to us!" "You go after Fearow," agreed Jenny.

Kellyn and Ash jumped on their waiting Dodrio and were gone, leaving Brock, Dawn, Solana and Jenny to pick a battle line-up to rival the opposition.
Jenny called on Growlithe while Brock summoned Croagunk.

"This isn't going to be easy," frowned Dawn. "I need everyone's help!"
In a flash Piplup, Buneary, Ambipom and Pachirisu were by the Co-ordinator's side.

Further down the canyon, Ash and Kellyn's Dodrio were gaining on the Fearow.
"Those stubborn pests," growled the client, glancing down at the courageous pair.
Ash urged his Dodrio on and the bird's great legs strode up the side of the canyon until it was high enough up to leap onto Fearow's back.
"Fury Attack!" yelled Kellyn.
Dodrio's beak pecked and pecked at Fearow until it fell out of the sky, crushing its cargo beneath it.

"Now give Riolu back!" ordered Ash.
"Not in a million years!" cried the crook, picking himself and Riolu up before limping into a cave. He disappeared down one of several dark passages then called on Aggron's Rock Smash move to fill the cave entrance with rocks.
For a moment Ash and Kellyn were stumped, until a Donphan lumbered into view. Kellyn used his Styler to capture it, harnessing its power to break up the rocks barring the cave.

Even then, there was a new challenge – the pair couldn't tell which passageway the client had taken! If they chose the wrong one, they might never catch him up and Riolu would be gone.

54

Meanwhile, Dawn, Brock, Jenny and Solana's Pokémon were doing their best to defend themselves against the monstrous Pokémon towering before them.
"They're way too strong!" said Dawn.
"How do we stand up to them?" asked Brock.
Luckily Solana was on hand to save the day. She pointed her Capture Styler at a nearby Trapinch, then shouted "Use Rock Tomb!" Massive boulders appeared, encircling and completely trapping the soldiers and their raging Pokémon.

In the cave Kellyn and Ash were having an equally rocky time of it.
"Boulders are blocking every passageway!" glared Kellyn. "And Riolu can only be in one of them."
But the Ranger had forgotten Ash and Riolu's aura connection. The Trainer closed his eyes and concentrated hard.
"This one!" called Ash, pointing to a passageway. "Riolu's in there!"
Once again Kellyn called on Donphan to clear the way and within moments the friends were out in the open.

The client couldn't believe his eyes as Ash and Kellyn appeared. Even so, he stubbornly refused to give up.

"Aggron!" he bellowed. "Double Edge!"

Kellyn retaliated using Donphan's Horn Attack and in the fray the client was knocked to the floor, releasing Riolu. Ash flicked the switch on the glass case transforming Riolu back from stone. As soon as it was free he gave the excited Pokémon a tight hug.

The client's last move – Aggron's Hyper Beam – just couldn't cut it against the awesome combination of Riolu's Aura Sphere and Pikachu's Volt Tackle.

It was all over.

In the canyon Dawn, Brock, Jenny and Solana congratulated themselves and their Pokémon on a job well done, as they tied the client's soldiers together. Hunter J had got away, but at least Riolu was safe.

As J's ship set a course for a new destination, Team Rocket still hadn't given up on their mission.

"Team Rocket to block!" cried Jessie as she steered their hot air balloon directly in the path of J's ship. Big mistake!

"Hey we're not through yet," protested Meowth. "Where'd you go?"

J's ship evaporated into thin air then took out the balloon and its occupants.

"We're blasting off again!" yelled the trio, as they spun away into the distance.

Ash and the gang had no idea Team Rocket
had even been involved in a plot.
"Mission safely accomplished!" said Kellyn
to Ash, Dawn and Brock.
"I told you Ash would be a big help,"
smiled Solana.
Ash blushed, but broke into a grin at the sight
of Riolu being finally reunited with its owner.
"On behalf of our kingdom I wish to convey my
sincere gratitude," said the old man. "Take care
Riolu," replied Dawn in a gentle voice.
"And take care of this," added Ash, handing
Riolu its doll.
Suddenly, to everyone's concern he clutched
his head in pain.
"That was just Riolu tellin' me thanks,"
grinned Ash.
Riolu nodded.
"I'm never gonna forget you!" added Ash.
"Not ever."

**NOT ONLY HAVE ASH AND HIS
FRIENDS SAVED A VERY SPECIAL RIOLU
FROM THE EVIL HUNTER J, THE FUTURE
OF AN ENTIRE KINGDOM HAS BEEN
SECURED. AND SO, WITH SO MANY
FOND MEMORIES OF AN AMAZING
ADVENTURE TO BRING ALONG WITH
THEM, OUR HEROES' SINNOH REGION
JOURNEY CONTINUES…**

AURA-READ LIKE ASH

Fighting-Type Pokémon Riolu is able to signal its emotions, feelings and even its location to others by projecting its aura. Talented Trainer Ash can read its thoughts, but in order to share his gift you'll need to hone your own mind-reading skills. Try this game with a friend!

1. Lay a 20p, 10p, 5p, 2p and 1p coin on a table, do not spend lots of time handling them beforehand.

2. Turn your back, and ask your friend to choose any coin.

3. Ask them to pick up the coin and hold it tightly in their hand for a few moments whilst concentrating on it.

4. Next, have them put the coin back on the table and move all of the coins around.

5. To find out which penny they chose, pick up each one and hold it against your forehead. Amaze them by telling them which one they chose.

To find out how to deduce the answer, turn to the Answers on page 68.

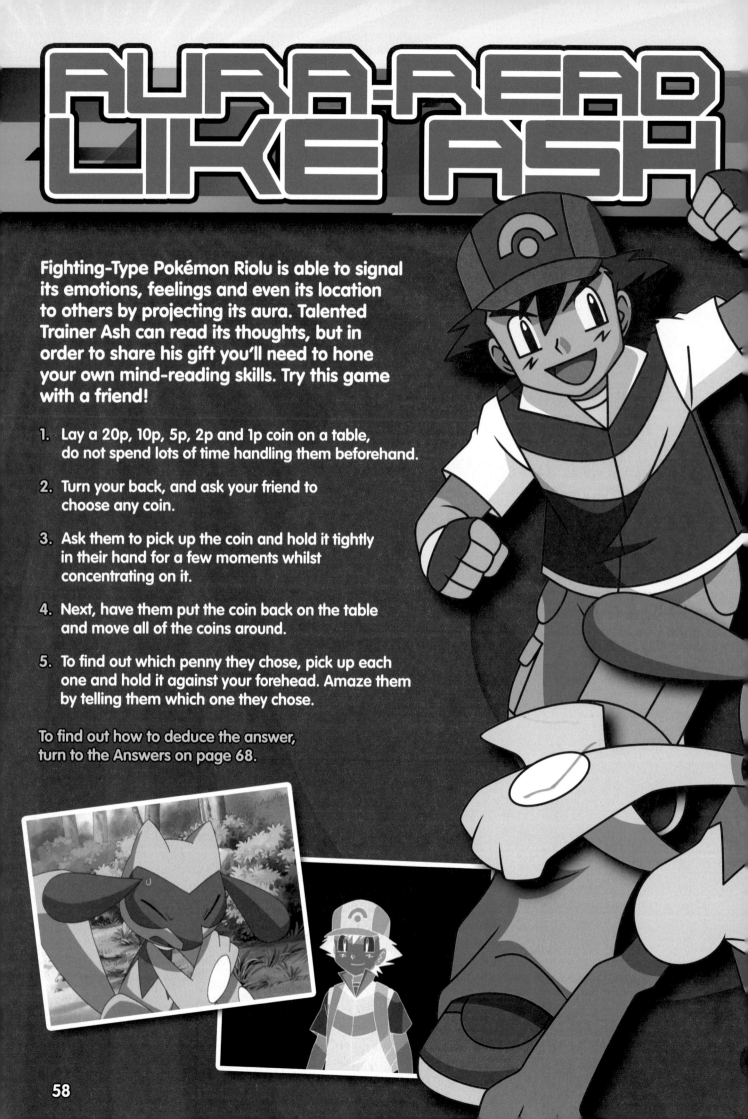

Check out this photo of Ash and Pikachu with their new friend, use it as a colouring guide for this awesome Pokémon picture!

ROCK N' ROLL GAME

Rock-Types make formidable foes – are you ready to enter their world? Find some Pokémon-crazy pals and pit the might of the Rock-Types against each other to see who comes out on top!

FOR 2-4 PLAYERS, YOU WILL NEED:
The Rock-Type stickers from the sticker sheet; A piece of sturdy card; Scissors; Dice.

49	50	51	52	53	54
48	47	46	45	44	43
25	26	27	28	29	30
24	23	22	21	20	19
START 1	2	3	4	5	6

GETTING READY

First take the stickers of Rock-Types Golem and Graveler, Geodude and Rampardos, (you'll need one per person playing) and stick them onto a piece of card. Cut round the Pokémon to make your pieces. Now line your Rock-Types up on the starting square and roll the dice. The highest number goes first.

HOW TO PLAY

Take turns to roll the dice and advance the number of squares shown. If you land on a fellow Rock-Type, move up the ladder. If however you land on a square featuring a member of Team Rocket or one of their Pokémon allies, you'll need to slide back down Seviper. Keep going – the first one to the finish line wins!

SINNOH POKÉDEX

STARAPTOR

TYPE:	NORMAL/FLYING
ABILITY:	INTIMIDATE
HEIGHT:	1.2m
WEIGHT:	24.9kg

Evolved from one of Ash's favourites, Staravia, Staraptor has a bold character. It will happily employ its talons and sharp beak to beat off much larger foes.

CHIMCHAR

TYPE:	FIRE
ABILITY:	BLAZE
HEIGHT:	0.5m
WEIGHT:	6.2kg

Although small in terms of average Pokémon, Chimchar is extremely agile. It easily scales cliffs and rock faces and thus is totally at home in the inhospitable mountainous Sinnoh terrain. Its fiery tail only goes out when it sleeps.

PHIONE

TYPE:	WATER
ABILITY:	HYDRATION
HEIGHT:	0.4m
WEIGHT:	3.1kg

Phione thrives in the temperate waters in and around the Sinnoh regions. It has no evolutions, but is said to have developed from groups of breeding Manaphy. Phione has a flotation sac on its head.

YANMEGA

TYPE:	BYG/FLYING
ABILITY:	SPEED BOOST/TINTED LENS
HEIGHT:	1.9m
WEIGHT:	51.5kg

This dragonfly-like Pokémon relies on speed to defend itself or retreat. When beating at top speed, its wings can strike with enough power to damage its opponent's internal organs.

DRIFLOON

TYPE:	GHOST/FLYING
ABILITY:	AFTERMATH/UNBURDEN
HEIGHT:	0.4m
WEIGHT:	1.2kg

This Pokémon is formed purely of the spirits of Pokémon and humans. It seeks out dank, humid places and prospers most during rainy seasons. Drifloon evolves into Drifblim.

HIPPOWDON

TYPE:	GROUND
ABILITY:	SAND/STREAM
HEIGHT:	2.0m
WEIGHT:	300.0kg

Gigantic Hippowdon uses ports on its body to blast enemies with internally stored sand, creating devastating twisters that reach several metres in height. Its first evolution is Hippopotas.

WHOSE EVOLUTION LINE IS IT ANYWAY?

1 SNOVER

2 PORYGON   PORYGON2

3   LUMINEON

4 GEODUDE   GRAVELER

WATCH OUT!
There's a red herring on this page? Which question is trying to trip you up and why?

A top breeder like Brock knows that most Pokémon come from a line of previous characters or are the first of several evolutions to come. Can you match his skill by completing the evolution chains using the stickers provided and identifying each one?

5 DUSKULL   DUSCLOPS   _____

6 _____   PRINPLUP   EMPOLEON

7 AIPOM   AMBIPOM   _____

8 _____   STARAVIA   STARAPTOR

QUICK QUIZ PART 2

AWESOME ACCURACY

Now you've tested your speed, this challenge is all about accuracy. There's no point in being the quickest to call your Pokémon to battle if you can't then get it to do the right move!

Answer these 10 questions as accurately as you can. You'll score 1 point for each element of your answer. Give yourself a further point if you get every part of the answer correct.

1 Two of Pikachu's signature moves are...

VOLT TAIL THUDB

2 Gible's two evolutions are...

POOTIN POOTIN

3 Legendary Sinnoh Pokémon include...

4 The notable attributes of Skuntank are...

5 The Team Rocket's names are...

6 Meowth is unusual because...

7 The seven basic types of Pokémon are...

8 The two humans who have lots of clones are...

9 Eevee's evolutions are...

10 Two Sinnoh slug-like Pokémon which have East and West Types are...

WHO DID YOU DO?

IF YOU SCORED BETWEEN 0-15

Back to the drawing board, a great Trainer needs to show deadly accuracy! Read through this book again and brush up on your Pokémon general knowledge, then get a friend or family member to test you.

IF YOU SCORED BETWEEN 15-25

Good work, you've demonstrated strong ability, you just need to work on the details. Make a list of your favourite Pokémon and write down every thing you can remember about them from appearance to moves and characteristics. This will help you retain the small, but vital details.

IF YOU SCORED 20+

CONGRATULATIONS. You could rival Brock with your encyclopaedic knowledge! You also share Ash's fantastic attention to detail. Work on your moves and you're assured a place in history as a top flight Trainer.

Page 11
PACHIRISU PAIRS
A and E

Pages 12-13
KETCHUM'S CROSSWORD

Page 28
RANGER IN DANGER

Page 29
WICKED WORDSEARCH

B	T	U	O	U	E	F	D	W	R	O
E	E	J	L	U	A	P	D	J	S	Q
N	F	X	O	T	S	U	D	P	E	U
I	F	C	F	J	B	A	A	S	V	D
V	U	H	A	A	M	J	Z	A	I	W
I	B	M	I	M	R	E	P	K	P	M
N	B	A	R	E	A	S	O	S	E	E
R	O	N	T	S	E	S	W	W	R	O
A	W	N	P	Z	P	I	V	A	T	A
C	U	A	F	T	M	E	J	R	E	H
H	I	N	N	A	V	O	I	G	S	S

Pages 32-33
QUICK QUIZ 1 - TIME TRIALS
1. YES
2. NO – it is an Ice-Type.
3. NO – it is Ketchum.
4. YES – one of the reasons why it's rarely sighted in Sinnoh.
5. NO – it rides on Ash's shoulder.
6. NO – it has two giant tusks.
7. NO – she is aided by Happiny's next evolution Chansey.
8. YES
9. NO – they met in Pewter City where Brock ran the Gym.
10. NO – the second type is pink and brown with yellow markings.
11. NO – it's Bronzong.
12. YES
13. NO – it has an inflatable collar to help its buoyancy.
14. NO – it stores electricity in its cheek pouches.
15. YES

Page 37
POKÉ DOT
Garchomp

Page 40
WHO DUNNIT?
1. Rules out Stunky.
2. Rules out Gliscor.
3. Rules out Purugly.
4. Rules out Tentacruel

Drapion is the culprit.

Page 41
SINNOH SILHOUETTES
1B.
2D.
3E.
4C.
5A.

Pages 58-59
AURA-READ LIKE ASH!
You will be able to tell which coin your friend chose by holding each up to your forehead – the one they picked and held will feel warmer than the others.

Pages 64-65
WHOSE EVOLUTIONARY LINE IS IT ANYWAY?
1. Snover, Abomasnow
2. Porygon, Porygon2, Porygon-Z
3. Finneon, Lumineon
4. Geodude, Graveler, Golem
5. Duskull, Dusclops, Dusknoir
6. Piplup, Prinplup, Empoleon
7. Aipom, Ambipom
8. Starly, Staravia, Staraptor

Number 7 is the red herring as Ambipom has no further evolutions. Infernape is the final form of Chimchar.

Pages 66-67
QUICK QUIZ PART 2 – AWESOME ACCURACY
1. Thunderbolt, Volt Tackle (score 1 for each, max score 3).
2. Gabite, Garchomp (score 1 for each, max score 3).
3. Palkia, Dialga, Giratina, Shaymin (score 1 for each, max score 5).
4. It squirts noxious fluid from the tip of its tail, it has a range of over 100 metres, it has purple and cream striped markings (score 1 for each, max score 4).
5. Jessie, James, Meowth (score 1 for each, max score 4).
6. It can speak and understand human language (score 1).
7. Fire, Grass, Water, Fighting, Electric, Psychic and Normal (score 1 for each, max score 8).
8. Nurse Joy and Officer Jenny (score 1 for each, max score 3).
9. Vaporeon, Flareon, Umbreon, Glaceon, Leafeon, Espeon, Jolteon (score 1 for each, max score 8).
10. Shellos and Gastrodon (score 1 for each, max score 3).